Tales Told in Tents

Stories from Central Asia

Written by
Sally Pomme Clayton

Illustrated by
Sophie Herxheimer

FRANCES LINCOLN CHILDREN'S BOOKS

Contents

ASIA

For my mother,
who could make anywhere home - S.P.C.

For my mother,
who brought me to the marvels of the imagination,
and for my daughter Rosa, who carries
the sparkly thread – S.H.

Tales Told in Tents copyright © Frances Lincoln Limited 2004
Text copyright © Sally Pomme Clayton 2004
Illustrations copyright © Sophie Herxheimer 2004

First published in Great Britain in 2004 by
Frances Lincoln Limited, 4 Torriano Mews
Torriano Avenue, London NW5 2RZ

www.franceslincoln.com

Distributed in the USA by Publishers Group West

British Library Cataloguing in Publication Data available on request

ISBN 1-84507-066-6

Set in Hiroshige Book and Albertus

Printed in Singapore
1 3 5 7 9 8 6 4 2

The Storyteller's Tale

When I was little, my sister and I used to throw a blanket over the washing line to make a tent. In the warm half-light we would set up camp, arranging beds and making a pretend fire. Then we would borrow one of Mum's saucepans, and sneak a handful of rice and raisins from the kitchen. We'd fill the saucepan with water from the hot tap and cook the rice and raisins over our fire, stirring the rice and stirring the rice until the water had turned white and starchy. It seemed as if we stirred for hours, and still the rice didn't cook. We'd eat it anyway, even though we knew we shouldn't, biting into the hard grains and chewing them for a long time. Then we'd curl up round the fire and tell stories. Days and nights passed in an afternoon. Finally, it really was bedtime. Dad would call us, the tent was pulled down and the blanket folded up.

We moved to a new house every two years or so. And each time we moved I wished we could take our house with us, just as people who live in tents carry their houses from place to place. Even though we couldn't carry our house, we could carry stories. Stories are light. You can carry them anywhere, pick more up along the way, and your load never gets heavier. So stories were a way of carrying the threads of our lives from place to place.

Later, when I started telling and collecting stories, I became interested in the nomadic cultures of Central Asia because of their rich storytelling traditions.

One summer I found myself sitting in a round felt tent, a yurt, on the steppes of southern Kazakhstan. Inside, the yurt was hung with silk and felt hangings. Quilts and carpets were placed in a horseshoe shape facing the yurt entrance. The women sat on one side of the tent, the men on the other, and the honoured guests in the middle. This horseshoe shaped seating arrangement is an important part of life throughout Central Asia. Many dinners I attended in houses and apartments followed the same seating pattern. It is called a dasturxan – which means both "tablecloth" and "hospitality".

Tea was served. It was drunk from small china bowls which were only a quarter filled. Huge samovars were always steaming, and the smoky, milky tea tasted absolutely divine. Once your bowl was empty, it was instantly refilled, which meant you only drank fresh, hot tea.

Food was generously offered. There was plaited bread, butter and cheese made from mare's milk, slivers of green pepper, dried apricots, fresh walnuts, and roasted lamb and horse meat.

Each piece of meat is a story that represents a different blessing to the eater. The meat from the horse's neck gives the eater strong shoulders for hard work. The stomach gives nourishment and health. The meat from between the horse's ribs is made into a special sausage. The ribs hold a horse together, and eating the rib meat holds the whole community together.

In between each mouthful toasts were drunk, holding up bowls of tea, shots of vodka, glasses of fizzy drinks, or bowls of frothy kumys – fermented mare's milk.

The toasts were beautiful, the language embroidered as intricately as a Kazakh coat. Toasts were made to guests, ancestors, storytellers, love and

the future. Stories were told, songs sung, and poems scribbled down and read hot from the page. The dasturxan is a place of nourishment for both body and heart.

Then we were served dishes of plov, the softest rice and raisins. I was sitting in a tent, with storytellers and poets, eating rice and raisins! I had stepped into my own story. I wasn't sure if I had found it or it had found me.

Central Asia is a vast area containing the countries Turkmenistan, Uzbekistan, Kazakhstan, Kyrgyzstan, Tadjikistan and Afghanistan. The landscape ranges from flat steppe land and deserts to mountains. The climate in this part of the world is extreme. The weather changes from scorching sun during the summer months to driving snow in winter. But nomadic tribes have developed an ingenious way of surviving: their felt tents keep them snug in winter, and cool in summer. Today some people still live nomadically, following their flocks of goats or sheep from pasture to pasture, carrying their houses and belongings with them.

In nomadic societies the storyteller is very important and stories are treasured. They are the gold you pass on to your children.

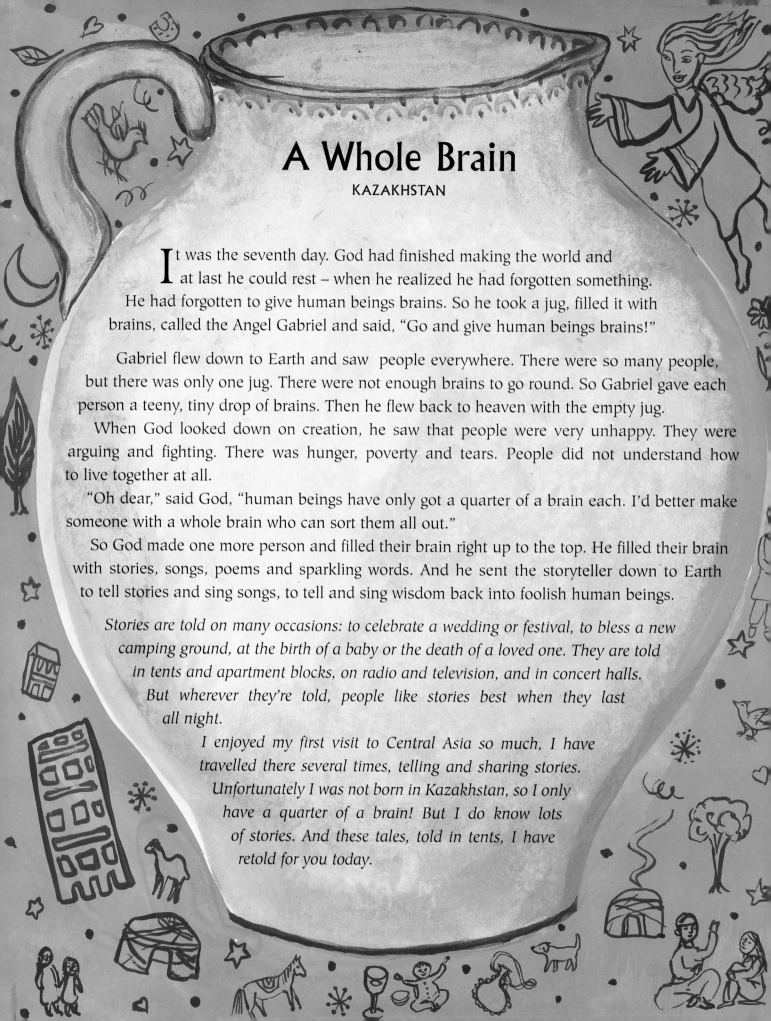

A Whole Brain

KAZAKHSTAN

It was the seventh day. God had finished making the world and at last he could rest – when he realized he had forgotten something. He had forgotten to give human beings brains. So he took a jug, filled it with brains, called the Angel Gabriel and said, "Go and give human beings brains!"

Gabriel flew down to Earth and saw people everywhere. There were so many people, but there was only one jug. There were not enough brains to go round. So Gabriel gave each person a teeny, tiny drop of brains. Then he flew back to heaven with the empty jug.

When God looked down on creation, he saw that people were very unhappy. They were arguing and fighting. There was hunger, poverty and tears. People did not understand how to live together at all.

"Oh dear," said God, "human beings have only got a quarter of a brain each. I'd better make someone with a whole brain who can sort them all out."

So God made one more person and filled their brain right up to the top. He filled their brain with stories, songs, poems and sparkling words. And he sent the storyteller down to Earth to tell stories and sing songs, to tell and sing wisdom back into foolish human beings.

Stories are told on many occasions: to celebrate a wedding or festival, to bless a new camping ground, at the birth of a baby or the death of a loved one. They are told in tents and apartment blocks, on radio and television, and in concert halls. But wherever they're told, people like stories best when they last all night.

I enjoyed my first visit to Central Asia so much, I have travelled there several times, telling and sharing stories. Unfortunately I was not born in Kazakhstan, so I only have a quarter of a brain! But I do know lots of stories. And these tales, told in tents, I have retold for you today.

The Secret of Felt

TURKMENISTAN

Every day the two brothers led their curly, black *Karaqul* sheep to the grasslands. As they climbed the slopes of the foothills to find fresh grass, they could see the *Karakum* desert in the distance, the sand dunes ridged like ocean waves. As they walked, the elder brother played a tune on his shepherd's pipe and the younger brother chewed some dry bread. Every now and then they stopped and called out to the flock. Sometimes they bent to pick berries, popping them into their mouths and sucking on the juice, or pulled up handfuls of herbs and tucked them into their pockets for their mother.

One day the younger brother stubbed his toe on a sharp stone.

"Ow, ow, ouch!" he shouted, leaping about.

"Let's have a look," said the elder brother, quickly pulling off his brother's boot. The toe was bleeding badly.

"Be careful, it hurts."

The elder brother had to stop the bleeding. So he reached over to one of the sheep, pulled some silky wool from its back and pressed it to his brother's foot.

"That feels better," sighed the younger brother. And the bleeding stopped. The brothers wrapped more wool tightly around the sore toe. Then the younger brother pulled on his boot. The wool was fluffy and made a soft cushion around his toe. By the time they arrived back at camp, the toe was better.

The boys put the sheep into their pen for the night, and their mother stirred the herbs they had gathered into the cooking pot.

"Mmmm, the stew smells good," said the boys, and they sat down by the fire to pull off their boots. But they found a strange thing: the wool around the younger brother's toe was not wool any more. The separate strands of wool had matted together into a thick, soft piece of material. The wool had turned into felt.

The boys looked at the wool. It had pressed together inside the boot as the younger brother had walked home. It had pressed together so tightly, it had become like a furry blanket.

The shepherd boys had made felt from wool, sweat and walking. They had discovered the secret of felt! Their mother was so proud, she ladled out an extra big bowl of steaming lamb stew for each of them.

Central Asian people kept the secret and have been making felt ever since.

Felt can be made from sheep's wool, goat-hair or camel's hair. The wool is beaten with sticks to separate the fibres. Then it is laid out on grass mats. Dyed wool can be laid on top to create patterns. Hot water is sprinkled on to the wool and the mats are rolled up tightly and tied. The roll is then pressed and pushed hard with arms, elbows, or feet, to compress the wool. Everyone joins in, pushing and pressing the roll for about two hours, singing songs and telling stories to make the work fun. When the roll is untied, the wool has matted together and become felt.

Felt is made into tents, wall-hangings, rugs, coats, hats and bags. One night I slept in a yurt in cosy luxury, lying on fluffy felt mattresses, surrounded by warm felt.

Felt is often decorated with intricate, curly patterns. The patterns have special names and are based on things people see around them every day.

RAM'S HORN

EAGLE'S WING

LITTLE HILL

GOOSE NECK

RAVEN'S CLAW

If you don't want to help us make felt, then don't come to our feast

KYRGYZ PROVERB

Blue Sky, White Wing

CENTRAL ASIA

It was ages ago
in the beginning.
You and I
were not in the world.
There was no grass or flowers
no berries or trees.
There was just
Sky and Earth.

Father Blue Sky
and Mother White Wing.
Tengri – blue sky
and Umai Ene – white wing.

In those days
blue sky stretched from one end to the other.
At that time
Mother Earth was half-woman half-bird
with one arm and one white wing.

White wing flashed against blue sky
wing brushed sky
and rain fell.
Soft rain fell like seeds.
Rain seeds fell to earth
and earth became green.

A tree grew
a giant tree grew.
The tree of all seeds
at the centre of the earth.
Its leaves touched heaven
and its roots pushed down
to the underworld.

Umai Ene sat in the tree
flapped her wing
and the seeds blew about.
Grass and flowers
berries and trees
you and I
came from the seeds.

Father Blue Sky
spread your tent
watch over us.
Mother White Wing
wrap your wing
protect us.

Tengri and Umai Ene are very old gods. Today Central Asian people follow Muslim, Jewish, Buddhist and Christian religions. But the old beliefs have not been forgotten – old and new live side by side. People still say, "May the Sky bless you", "May the Earth hold you". And in Kyrgyzstan I found Umai Ene! She has become a felt pattern: a curve with a sweeping wing on one side and a stubby arm on the other. The pattern is called "Half-bird Half-woman".

The sky is your father, the earth is your mother

CENTRAL ASIAN SAYING

The Girl who Cried a Lake

KYRGYZSTAN

*I*lgeri Ilgeri, there was a *Khan* who was head of the Wolf clan, and he had the most beautiful daughter.

She was graceful, like a tree blowing in the breeze, with long black plaits and rosy red cheeks. But she was unusual, because her eyes were bright blue, like burning hot sapphires.

Many Kyrgyz boys wanted to marry the girl with hot blue eyes.

One day, the girls of the Wolf clan decided to play *kesh-kumay* – kiss-chase on horseback! The girls leapt on to their horses, holding whips in their hands, and sped across the *steppe*. The boys chased them like cowboys, with red and yellow scarves tied round their heads, leaning on the necks of their horses, urging them to go faster. If a boy caught a girl and kissed her, then it was said they would marry.

The riders chased each other, their horses kicking up earth, steam snorting from their nostrils. The riders tried to trick each other, turning their horses sharply and changing direction. Suddenly a young hunter galloped across the steppe. He caught the Khan's daughter and kissed her rosy cheek. She was surprised, and laughed. The hunter bent and picked a posy of wild bright flowers for the girl, and they began to talk. Then all their young friends gathered round and cheered.

"What's going on?" asked the Khan, stepping out of his yurt.

"The hunter caught your daughter," everyone shouted. "They will marry."

The Khan looked at the hunter.

"I don't think so," he said.

"But Father," said the girl, "he won the chase."

"You can't marry that bandit," said her father. "He has nothing. He lives in the mountains with an eagle on his wrist, hunting rabbits and looking for snow-leopards. He doesn't own a thing."

The Khan's daughter stepped forward, "But he is bold and brave, Father. He's a skilled rider. He knows the ways of the land and can follow the invisible tracks left by animals."

"Get inside," said her father, pointing at the yurt. "I'll hear no more of it."

⊕

But the Khan's daughter and the hunter could not forget each other. They met secretly whenever they could. The girl would ride up to the *jailoo*, the grassy pastures on the lower slopes of the mountains. There the hunter would give her fresh milk from his horse, tell her stories about the mountains, and they would look at the ever-changing, rushing sky.

"Please, Father," she said one day, "we have fallen in love. He may not own much, but he can hear trees speaking and knows what rivers are saying."

"No," said her Father. "You will marry the Khan's son from the Vulture clan, across the valley."

"But I don't want to."

"It's a powerful match, and will keep the peace."

So preparations for the wedding began. Mare's milk was poured into leather bags, shaken, and left to ferment, to make the festive milky drink *kumys*. Tents were put up, and horses given new saddles. Piles of fresh flat bread were made, sheep roasted, and platters of fruit and nuts arranged.

Then the Khan's daughter was dressed for her wedding. Her mother helped her into a red silk dress and a long embroidered waistcoat. Heavy silver necklaces were placed over her head, silver bracelets reached all the way up her arms. And a tall hat was placed on her head, with braids dangling from the brim like a thousand tiny plaits, each braid decorated with a glass bead that jangled as she walked.

"You look like a princess!" sighed her mother.

But the girl began to cry. A hot, blue tear squeezed out of her eye. She tried to wipe it away, but more tears came. Her throat was dry and sore, and she could not stop the tears rolling down her cheeks. Big fat blue tears poured from her eyes. Tears poured from her blue eyes, rolled down her cheeks, and dripped on to her dress.

She could not stop crying. The tears came faster and faster. The girl cried so much, she cried a stream. She cried a river. She cried a lake of tears. The girl cried a lake of tears that completely covered up the Wolf clan and the Vulture clan. Everyone – her mother, father and friends, her husband and all his people – sank down under the waves. All that was left was a big blue lake.

The hunter rode down from the mountains, and found a lake. Where the valley had been, was a sapphire lake. He looked into the water,

"It's so blue. Like the eyes of my girl."

He cupped his hands, filled them with water, and drank.

"The water's warm. And it tastes salty, like tears."

The hunter stared at the blue lake.

"It *is* my girl. She has become a lake!"

Then he stretched his arms above his head,

"How I wish I could be the highest mountain," he cried, pushing his arms up higher, "then I could look into her blue eyes for ever."

Suddenly the hunter found himself growing, reaching higher and higher into the sky. Up and up he stretched, until he was higher than all the other mountains. He had become the highest mountain of all, covered in snow, looking down into the blue lake. Looking down into the hot blue eyes of his beloved. The mountain looked into the lake, and the lake gazed up at the mountain.

The mountain and the lake are still there, looking at each other, and can never be parted.

Lake Issyk-Kul is a vast blue lake in Kyrgyzstan. Issyk means "hot", and Kul means "lake". Issyk-Kul – Hot Lake. If you dip your toe into the lake you will find the water is warm. Hot tears warm the lake and make it salty. Even though the lake is far, far from the sea, it is salty. And because it is salty, it never freezes in winter, even when the ground is thick with snow.

Lake Issyk-Kul is surrounded by high snow-capped mountains, the Tian-Shan – "Celestial Mountains". They are so high that sometimes the bottom of the mountains disappear because they are shrouded in mist. Then you only see the snowy peaks, and the mountains really do look like celestial mountains, mountains floating in heaven.

Issyk-Kul is a place for travellers and poets. Lie on its sandy beaches, dream over its gentle waves. Dive into the warm water and gaze up at the heavenly white peaks.

Every rock, river, track and hill in Kyrgyzstan has a story. Many of the stories describe how human beings were turned into part of the landscape. So the land is actually made of stories. Stories that remind Kyrgyz people where they have come from. Tales that tell us nature is alive.

I didn't sleep much one night, in a lonely gorge, listening to the wind and the rushing river. I couldn't help feeling that out there, in the dark, were all kinds of strange, invisible beings.

The world's eye is Issyk-Kul, the world's back-bone the Tian-Shan

KYRGYZ PROVERB

The Carpet of Dreams
AFGHANISTAN

At the end of a twisting passageway, in the city of old Herat, was a tiny carpet shop. It smelled of wool. There was wool waiting to be dyed, wool hanging from the ceiling to dry, wool being woven on looms and finished carpets piled high. It was where Arif and his mother and father lived.

"I hate weaving!" grumbled Arif. "I've broken another thread."

"Go and get a breath of fresh air," said his mother, "then start again."

"I don't want to be a weaver, I want to be a merchant and ride on the back of a camel and travel the Silk Road!"

"Oh Arif, you're such a dreamer. And you're too young to travel. Anyway, Father and I need you here."

Arif was always dreaming about travelling the Silk Road, crossing mountains and deserts to Samarkand. But his father would shake his head and say, "I wanted a son who would be a carpet-weaver, not a merchant."

One afternoon Arif lay down on an old carpet at the back of the shop, yawned, and fell asleep. He began to dream. He was riding a camel laden with carpets through the gates of an unknown city. He bowed before a shining princess, gave her a carpet and she placed a ruby in his hand.

"Wake up, Arif!" cried his father, shaking him. "There's work to be done."

Arif blinked and stretched. Then he saw something glinting in the palm of his hand.

"Oh! Look, Father," he cried in surprise. And he told his father the dream. They could hardly believe their eyes. Arif's father examined the jewel. It was a ruby!

"This is a sign, Arif," he said. "Take the ruby, and see where it leads. You can always sell it if you need to."

Then Arif's father rolled up the carpet his son had been sleeping on.

"Take the carpet as well. It seems to be a carpet of dreams."

⟡

Early next morning, Arif climbed on to the back of a camel. He watched the merchants tying up their loads of silk and spices and did the same, rolling up his carpet and tying it to his saddle. Then the camel train headed out of the city towards the Silk Road. Arif's mother and father waved goodbye, wondering if they would ever see their son again.

Arif felt on top of the world on top of his camel. They joined the Silk Road and travelled west towards Persia. It was dusty. The camels wound their way along high passes and through rocky ravines. Arif listened as the merchants talked about the best trade routes, how to spot a bargain, and catch a thief.

At sunset they came to a *caravanserai*.
The old stone inn was surrounded by camels and
horses. Arif tied up his camel and went inside.
There were merchants speaking languages he had
never heard. Some had spread out rolls of silk,
boxes made of jade, delicate china tea-cups, and
were haggling over prices. Others fed their
animals, dipped bread into spicy stew, told
stories or fell asleep by the fire.

Arif spread out his carpet. Away from
his father's shop, it looked different.
The carpet glowed a deep red, and
the white pattern of almond
blossom seemed to float on the
surface like a dark night
sprinkled with stars.

A man wearing very expensive robes bent and admired the carpet.

"This is good enough for royalty," he said, and offered Arif a bag of gold.

That night Arif fell asleep, the bag of gold under his pillow, the ruby in his hand, thinking, 'I am a real merchant, travelling the real Silk Road!'

And so Arif became a merchant. He returned home to his amazed parents and loaded up a camel with more of their carpets. He travelled east to China, south to India, back and forth selling carpets. People thought the carpets were so beautiful, they wanted more. And all the time Arif kept the ruby in his pocket. He never sold it, but would turn it over in his fingers and think of the princess in his dream.

✛

At last Arif travelled north to Uzbekistan, and reached the city of Samarkand. He wandered through the huge city gates, past towering minarets and blue-domed mosques to the *bazaar*. It was bustling with shoppers, and merchants called out their wares,

"Sandalwood and jasmine perfume, fresh from India…"

"Best embroidered coats…"

"Gold and amber earrings, buy before they're gone…"

Arif unrolled his carpets. At once a man appeared and bowed.

"Your presence is requested at the palace," he said solemnly.

Arif recognized him. It was the man with the expensive robes. Arif followed him through the streets to the palace. Inside it was cool and quiet: there were tinkling fountains, shady balconies and turquoise tiles. Arif suddenly felt he was not dressed properly, and when they came to the throne room, he tried to brush the dust from his clothes.

"Princess Yulduz," announced the man.

Arif gasped. Sitting on a golden throne was a shining princess. It was the princess from his dream! And behind her, hanging on the wall, was his father's carpet, the carpet that looked like a dark night sprinkled with stars.

"Who made this carpet?" asked Princess Yulduz.

"My father."

"It is very beautiful," she replied. "Except for one thing. It has a mistake. Look, here… the pattern doesn't match."

"It's not a mistake," smiled Arif. "My father always weaves one little mistake into his carpets on purpose."

"But why would you make a mistake on purpose?" exclaimed the princess.

"It's a tradition," said Arif. "My father's carpets are perfect, but he weaves one mistake into them on purpose, to show that only God can make something that's completely perfect."

Princess Yulduz looked at the carpet with delight.

"A perfect mistake!" she laughed.

"Yulduz," said Arif. "What does it mean?"

"It means 'star'," replied the princess.

"That is the perfect name for you. Would you accept my gift?" And he held out the ruby.

"Where did you get that?" cried Princess Yulduz. "I lost it ages ago, and I've been looking for it ever since!"

Arif looked at the princess in amazement.

"The ruby led me to you," he said. Then he told her all about his dream, and how he became a merchant.

Princess Yulduz gazed at the carpet.

"It must be a magic carpet," she said. "It makes your dreams come true."

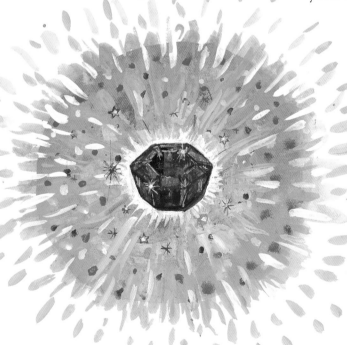

Arif married Princess Yulduz. And even though he became a king, he could not stop travelling. So Princess Yulduz climbed on to her camel and travelled the Silk Road with him to old Herat.

Outside the carpet shop, Arif's father hugged his son tightly.

"I'm so proud of you. I was wrong, it was not a mistake to have a son who wanted to be a merchant. It was a blessing. And now I have a perfect daughter as well."

As for the carpet of dreams and the ruby, Arif and Yulduz took great care of them and gave them to their children, who gave them to their children, who...

I'm not sure where the carpet and ruby are now. Perhaps they are further along the Silk Road. And maybe you will fall asleep on the carpet of dreams next...

A network of Silk Roads criss-cross Central Asia, stretching from China to Turkey. Traders once travelled along the roads, buying and selling goods at cities and caravanserai along the way.

I travelled on the Silk Road in Southern Kyrgyzstan, near the border with China. We bumped along in a truck, down a dried-up river bed, winding our way into the mountains through a landscape that looked as if it hadn't changed since the beginning of time. Nestling in the mountains was a dark stone building, Tash Rabat, an 11th-century caravanserai.

Tash Rabat was the last stop before China, a welcome place of rest, food and shelter. Under a domed roof was a hall with a central fire surrounded by stone benches. I imagined travellers sitting round the fire sharing stories of their different ways of life. The silent walls seemed thick with tales, and I felt close to those ghostly travellers, their stories still travelling across the world hundreds of years later.

Unroll your carpet and I shall see what is written on your heart

AFGHAN SAYING

Riddle Bazaar
UZBEKISTAN

Made from a worm
but soft and light,
keeps you cool in the day
and warm at night.

Sweet little princess
with a crown on her head,
break her open
and her jewels are red.

All is white,
a table-cloth,
soft eiderdown,
a sea of froth.

Round as globes,
from the earth they peep,
when they shed their robes
they make us weep.

Always restless,
always free,
can open doors
and fell a tree.

One eye
and a sharp tooth.

Silver cradle,
Silver plate,
Silver necklace,
Silver face.

Wearing clothes
when it's hot,
going naked
when it's not!
Funny way
to dress, I say.

The answers can be found on page 57

The Bag of Trickness

KAZAKHSTAN

Erte, erte, ertede, Aldar-Kose was walking across the steppe. He was cold. The ground was covered in thick snow, and his coat had seventy holes and ninety patches.

Suddenly he heard the sound of horse's hooves. Riding towards him on a fine horse was a rich man wearing a fur hat, fur coat and big furry mittens. Aldar-Kose quickly undid his holey old coat and began to hum a little tune:

> "I'm so lucky,
> I'm so happy,
> I'm so warm today!
> I'm so lucky..."

The rich man pulled up his horse.

"Excuse me," he said, "how can you be warm in a coat full of holes?"

"Aha!" laughed Aldar-Kose. "This is no ordinary coat, this is a magic coat. The wind blows in through one hole and out through another, and I stay toasty, toasty warm inside."

The rich man's mouth fell open.

"Well, that's amazing!" he said. "Is your coat for sale?"

"Never," said Aldar-Kose.

"I'd give you a bag of gold."

Aldar-Kose shook his head. "This coat was a gift from my grandfather.

There is only one like it in the whole world. Anyway, I'd freeze without this coat."

"What if I give you a bag of gold, and my coat as well?" said the rich man.

"Throw in your hat and mittens, and it's a deal," replied Aldar-Kose.

So the rich man gave Aldar-Kose the gold, his coat, his hat and his mittens. And Aldar-Kose gave the rich man his coat with seventy holes and ninety patches.

"Take great care of it," said Aldar-Kose. "That coat's unique."

Then Aldar-Kose pulled on the warm furs, tucked the gold into his pocket and walked away as fast as he could.

The rich man put on the holey old coat and waited for the wind to blow in through one hole and out of another. He began to shiver. His teeth chattered. The wind blew in through one hole, in through another hole, and in through another. The wind blew in through seventy holes! He was freezing!

But Aldar-Kose was toasty, toasty warm. He went to his friends' yurt, called for some tea and began to boast.

"Be careful, Aldar-Kose," warned his friends, "that rich man will want his coat back."

"Ha!" laughed Aldar-Kose. "He's so stupid, I could trick him again."

Just then, the rich man burst into the yurt.

"This coat doesn't work!" he cried.

"Oh dear," said Aldar-Kose, scratching his head. "I've just remembered, my grandfather said the magic would only work for me."

"I want my coat back," said the rich man.

"A deal's a deal," said Aldar-Kose.

"You tricked me!" shouted the rich man.

"But I couldn't have tricked you. I wasn't carrying my bag of trickness."

The rich man's mouth fell open.

"What's a bag of trickness?"

"It's where I keep my tricks. I can't trick anyone without my bag of trickness. I'd show it to you, but," sighed Aldar-Kose, "it's at home and I can't fetch it because I haven't got a horse."

"Borrow my horse," said the rich man. "I want to see that bag."

✤

Aldar-Kose rode home on the rich man's horse. Outside his yurt he tied the horse up, took out his hunting knife, and cut off the horse's long tail. Then he went to the flour bin and filled his pockets full of flour.

Aldar-Kose walked back across the steppe. Not far from his friends' yurt, he dug a hole in the snow. He buried the horse's tail in the ground, leaving a tiny bit of hair poking up through the snow. Then he patted his face with flour and stepped into the yurt.

His friends jumped up.

"What's happened, Aldar-Kose?" they cried. "You look as if you've seen a ghost."

"That horse is possessed by a demon," shuddered Aldar-Kose.

"Rubbish," said the rich man, "you're trying to trick me. Where's the bag?"

"I haven't got it," said Aldar-Kose. "You see, I was riding home, when your horse suddenly reared up in the air, turned round three times and spoke in a human voice. It said, 'Master, I'm coming home.' There was a rumbling sound, the earth opened up and your horse disappeared under the ground!"

The rich man's mouth fell open,

"How can a horse disappear under the ground?"

"I'll show you," said Aldar-Kose.

He led the rich man across the snow.

"There's his tail," said Aldar-Kose, pointing to the horsehair sticking up through the snow.

The rich man grabbed hold of the horse's tail and began to pull.

"That's it," cried Aldar-Kose. "Pull harder, you might get him back."

The rich man pulled, and pulled, and pulled the tail right out of the ground.

"Oh dear," cried Aldar-Kose, "you've pulled off his tail. You'll never get him back now."

The rich man wiped the tears from his eyes.

"My poor horse, possessed by demons. I'd better bury his tail."

And so they buried the tail. And Aldar-Kose placed a little sign on top of the grave that said, "Here lies a tail."

And a very good tale it was too. Aldar-Kose went home that night and was pleased with his bag of trickness. He was warm, he was rich, and his horse soon grew a new tail.

There are many stories about the trickster Aldar-Kose. His tricks always get him out of trouble. But the best trick he ever played was when he married Shigai-Bai's lovely daughter. I'll tell you that story next time.

Zarina's Orchard
TADJIKISTAN

It was dry and dusty. There was no water. Nothing would grow and everyone was thirsty. Zarina and her thirty-nine sisters picked up their empty jugs and walked over the mountain to the river. They filled their jugs at the river, then began the long walk home, careful not to spill a drop of precious water.

"Oh," sighed Zarina.

"Oh, oh, oh," sighed her thirty-nine sisters. "It's such hard work carrying water!"

"If only we could bring the river to us," said Zarina, "instead of us going to the river."

The next day, while the sisters were filling their jugs, the great hunter Feridun passed by.

"What are you doing?" he asked.

"Our land is dry," said Zarina. "We have to fetch water every day."

"If only we could bring the river to us," sighed the thirty-nine sisters, "instead of us going to the river."

"I have thirty-nine brothers," said Feridun. "Maybe we can help."

The next morning, Feridun and his thirty-nine brothers began work. They hacked and chipped and hacked and chipped at the mountain for thirty-eight days. On the thirty-ninth day they reached the other side. And on the fortieth day, water gushed through. They had brought the river to Zarina and her sisters!

At last there was water to drink, crops began to grow and everyone could wash their clothes.

✢

Zarina walked along the banks of the new river, "I will never get tired of looking at this water," she said happily.

Suddenly there was a flash of light. Standing before her was an old man with white hair, a beard, and a robe of shining green silk the colour of spring.

"Zarina," he said. "This is for you." And he handed her a bag of seeds.

"Scatter the seeds along the river bank. But don't look back. Don't look back until you have scattered all the seeds."

Zarina took the bag, and was about to say 'who are you?', when the old man vanished.

Zarina walked along the river bank scattering the seeds. When the bag was nearly empty, she was filled with a desire to look back. Before she could stop herself, she had turned her head. And what a sight met her eyes! Trees, bushes, flowers and plants had sprung up from the seeds.

Zarina ran back along the river. The desert had become an orchard. There were red apples and sweet cherries, juicy plums and ripe apricots, fresh almonds and green walnuts. And there was one small tree which had round ruby-red fruit with a little crown on top. Zarina broke open the fruit. Inside there were glowing red seeds. She squeezed the seeds into her mouth and drank the juice. Delicious! It was a pomegranate.

Zarina looked about. There was only one pomegranate tree.

"What a shame," she said. Then she looked at the seeds left in the bag. "More pomegranate seeds!"

As Zarina scattered the seeds, a ripple of wind caught them, blew them into the river, and the seeds were washed away.

Then Zarina remembered what the old man had said: "Don't look back until you have scattered all the seeds."

But it was too late. She had looked back, and now there would only ever be one pomegranate tree.

✛

Zarina's thirty-nine sisters and Feridun's thirty-nine brothers ran to the river. They admired the trees, gobbled up the fruit and nuts, drank the sweet pomegranate juice, and wished there were more pomegranate trees.

Suddenly they heard a rumbling sound. A wind whipped up. Dust began to blow, and the sky went black. The brothers and sisters clung to each other. A whirlwind swirled, curled and settled on the river bank. And out stepped a *Dev*. A terrible, evil Dev. A Dev with a bald head, one red eye, a long black tongue, a hairy belly, hairy legs and long, bony fingers.

"How dare you turn my desert into an orchard!" he boomed. "Dust and dry it shall be, dust and dry it shall stay."

And the Dev began to blow. Dust poured out of his nostrils and blew across the orchard. Dust covered everything. The Dev whirled away in his whirlwind, but the dust blew without stopping.

Everyone ran home, closed their doors, shut their windows and kept their animals inside.

"Oh, oh, oh!" said the thirty-nine sisters. "What shall we do?"

"We must stop him," said Zarina.

"It's impossible," said the sisters. "Devs can change their shape into anything they like."

"Then we must kill him."

"Devs can't be killed: their heart is not in their body."

"Well, where is their heart?" asked Zarina.

"No one knows. Oh, oh, oh!" cried the sisters.

The storm raged, sand blew over the orchard and dust filled up the river. Zarina listened to the wind and thought, "No one is going to turn my orchard into a desert."

That night Zarina crept out of bed, pulled on her clothes and went out into the dark. Dust blew into her eyes and mouth, and up her nose. She covered her face with a scarf and struggled through the wind to the river bank. Suddenly there was a flash of light. It was the old man dressed in green.

"Bold Zarina," he said, "a Dev's heart is inside an egg, inside a dove, inside a bag, under his pillow. Crack the egg and you will kill the Dev. But when you crack the egg, don't look back. Whatever you do, don't look back."

Zarina was about to say 'thank you', but the old man vanished.

Zarina pushed on, through the wind and dust, up the mountain. The dust was blowing from a dark cave.

"This must be where the Dev lives," she shuddered, and pulled the scarf tighter over her nose. She felt her way into the cave. In the darkness she could hear the Dev snoring. He was asleep, but with every snore, dust streamed from his nostrils, turning the orchard into a desert.

Zarina lay down on the cave floor, and crawled beneath the stream of dust. She crawled to the Dev's bed, and slowly pushed her hand under the Dev's pillow. There was a bag with something fluttering inside.
She grasped it and pulled.

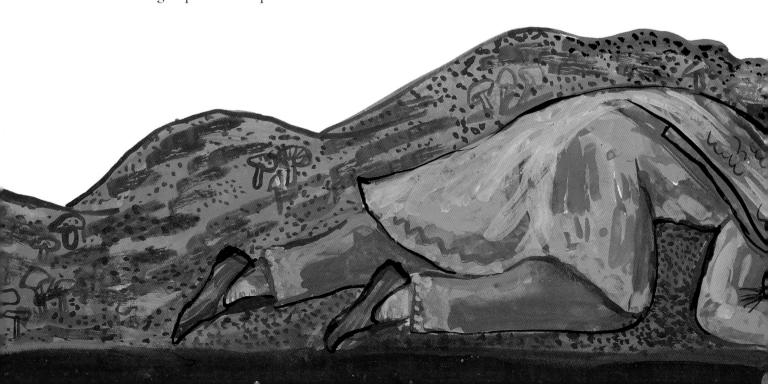

The Dev rolled over. Zarina held her breath and stayed as still as she could. Then gently, gently, she began to pull the bag. The Dev twitched and grunted. Zarina pulled and pulled and pulled the bag from under his pillow. Then she leapt to her feet and ran.

"Give me my heart!" shouted the Dev, and lumbered out of bed after her.

Zarina ran, and as she ran, she opened the bag. A white dove fluttered into her hands...

"I want my heart!" roared the Dev.

...And the dove laid an egg in Zarina's hand. The Dev stretched out his long bony fingers,

"That's mine!" he cried.

Zarina cracked the egg. And as it broke, the Dev met his death. His heart cracked. There was a rumbling and a trembling, a moaning and a groaning. But what happened to the Dev, I cannot tell you, because this time Zarina did not look back.

At once the storm stopped, and it began to rain. It rained and rained and all the dust was washed away. Zarina's orchard was green again.

Everyone ran to the river bank. They were so happy, they had a party. And the party turned into a wedding, because Zarina married Feridun.

The thirty-nine sisters and the thirty-nine brothers raised their glasses and drank to the health of Zarina and Feridun, who brought the river through a mountain and turned the desert into an orchard. But the brothers and sisters were careful not to drink too much – because they only had a little pomegranate juice.

Zarina looked and looked for the old man dressed in green, but she never saw him again. Who was he? Look carefully, and you might see him again, among these pages.

Water and trees are precious throughout Central Asia, and when a tree has roots that go down into running water, it becomes a wish-tree. Whenever I passed a wish-tree, I would stop my journey and, like other travellers, tie a handkerchief or strip of cloth to the branches of the tree and make a wish. Then I would carry on down the road, leaving my wish behind and the wish-tree decorated with fluttering ribbons of prayers.

The Heart of your Friend

KAZAKHSTAN

The heart of your friend is a mirror.
Don't mark the mirror,
your own face will look dirty.

The heart of your friend is a river.
Don't spit in the river,
some day you will be thirsty.

The heart of your friend is a *dombra*.
Don't tune the instrument too tightly,
the strings might break.

The heart of your friend is as vast as the steppe.
Don't try to contain it,
you might find yourself in prison.

The heart of your friend is a mountain top
where golden eagles make their nests.
There you will be
face to face with the sun.

*This poem is based on a Kazakh folksong, sung by
an elegant old lady while she played the* dombra – *the Kazakh lute.*

Only songs can cover the vastness of the steppe

KAZAKH SAYING

Father of Stories, Horse of Songs

CENTRAL ASIA

Oh my Khan,
under blue skies
beneath spreading trees
beside swift rivers
surrounded by strong horses
sitting on carpets of felt,
our ancestors drank tea.

In this time, Korkut was a young man. He was just sixteen years old when he had a dream. He dreamt that Death was looking for him.

Korkut woke with a start. "I am too young to die!" he cried. "Death can take me when I'm old. Death can take me when I'm ready." And he leapt on to his beautiful chestnut horse.

"Carry me, horse," he cried, "carry me away from Death."

Korkut had not ridden far when he came to some people digging a hole in the ground.

"What are you digging?" he asked.

"We are digging the grave of Korkut," they replied.

Korkut turned his horse and rode in the other direction. He came to some more people digging a hole.

"What are you digging?"

"We're digging the grave of Korkut."

Korkut rode fast. But everywhere he rode, there were people with spades, digging his grave.

48

Korkut did not stop riding. The chestnut horse galloped through sun and wind, stars and snow, looking for a place where there was no Death.

Korkut asked a tree, "Do you know the place where there is no Death?"

"Death is here," whispered the tree. "Birds peck me, leaves fall from me."

Korkut asked the steppe, "Do you know the place where there is no Death?"

"Death is here," moaned the steppe. "Sheep graze me, horses' hooves pound me."

Korkut asked the mountain, "Do you know the place where there is no Death?"

"Death is here," rumbled the mountain. "Rain lashes me, wind howls around me."

✤

Suddenly Korkut's horse stumbled. Its legs gave way and it fell to the ground. The chestnut horse was worn out. Korkut ran to the river to fetch water, but the horse was too tired to drink. Korkut watched as his beautiful horse closed its eyes and died.

"Death is here," wept Korkut. And he buried his face in his horse's mane. "My beloved horse, there must be a place where there is no Death."

Korkut took his knife and cut a branch from a tree. He began to carve a pear-shaped box. He stripped some skin from his horse and stretched it over the box. He twisted hairs from his horse's mane into two long strings, and tied them to each end of the box. Then he cut hair from his horse's tail, and stretched it along a stick.

Korkut made a musical instrument, a horsehair fiddle and a horsehair bow.

Korkut waded into the river and stood on a stone. He rested the fiddle in the cuff of his boot and began to play. He drew the horsehair bow across the strings. Music filled the air. Korkut began to sing a song about the life and death of his beautiful chestnut horse. The sound of Korkut's music echoed across the steppe.

Children stopped playing, old men stopped working, women put down their embroidery. They all ran to the river and stood silently, listing to Korkut's music.

Korkut sang of warriors and princesses, eagles and wolves. The horsehair fiddle resounded and everything listened. The rocks listened. The wind fell silent. The river stopped babbling. The birds were still. The flowers moved closer. All creation listened to Korkut's songs.

At the back of the crowd there was a shadowy figure. It was Death. Death had come to listen to Korkut's music. Death listened in wonder as Korkut sang of heroes and monsters, saints and devils and magic horses. Korkut sang and sang, and Death listened. Death was so entranced by the stories, he forgot his work. And all the time that Korkut sang, nobody died. Korkut's songs and stories held back death.

Many, many years passed. And there was no death. Korkut grew old, his hair turned white and his back bent.

"Now I am ready," said Korkut. He stepped out of the river, put his instrument on the ground at the feet of all the people who had been listening, and let Death take him.

The people buried Korkut on the banks of the river. Then they picked up his horsehair fiddle and began to play. They sang his stories and played his tunes. Korkut and his horse lived on, in the place where there is no death – the place of stories.

The people called the horsehair fiddle the *kobiz*. And they carved a horse's head on top of the kobiz, remembering how the horse of songs helped make the first fiddle.

Korkut's grave is on the banks of the Syr Darya river, in Southern Kazakhstan. And it is said that if you sleep beside Korkut's grave, you will become a poet.

Korkut became known as Dede Korkut, Father Korkut, father of all the stories he had created – stories still being sung by storytellers today.

Dede Korkut sang the stories
of all the Central Asian peoples.
Like them,
we come to this world and leave it,
camp and move on.
For if we did not die
the earth would not be made.
When Death comes
may he give you fair passage.
May your firm-rooted mountain never crumble.
May your great shady tree never be cut down.
May your clear-flowing river never run dry.
May your horse never stumble.
May your sword never be notched in the fray.
May your lamp,
which God has lit,
never be put out.
Oh my Khan.

I climbed on to Kara's back. His name meant "black" and he was black. Kyrgyz horses are known for their strength and ability to climb steep slopes. A silver whip was placed in my hand, and I was shown how to hold the reins Kyrgyz-style, like a cowgirl, reins in one hand and whip in the other. Then we set off, up a mountain!

To make a horse go, riders cry, "Chuu up, chuu up". To make a horse stop, they say, "'Dddrrrr".

I didn't like to use the whip. But as we climbed higher and the horses waded through streams and scrambled up rocks, I learned how important the whip is for Kyrgyz people. The whip is called a kamchy. It is made of leather, with a handle of wood or bone decorated with silver. If you lose your kamchy, it is very bad luck. Whips are hung in a special place beside the door. Whips are used gently. And I learned that by softly tapping the horse on its flank, I could communicate with Kara.

We rode up to the jailoo, the cool green pastures. The horses rested, and we fetched water from a stream, made a fire from fir-cones and boiled tea in a samovar.

On the way back, I was glad I had learned how to use a kamchy. Kara left the path and galloped off towards his farm, quite the wrong direction for me! But my kamchy helped me tell Kara where I wanted to go.

When we arrived home, I gave Kara a piece of apple and hung the kamchy up beside the door.

Horses are a hero's wings

KYRGYZ SAYING

The Fountain of Life
CENTRAL ASIA

Oh, but eternal life *does* exist!

One day an old man was deep in prayer, when he heard a fluttering sound. He opened his eyes and there was a bird. A rare bird, with red and gold wings. The bird shook her feathers, they fell to the ground, and out stepped a girl, a lovely girl with dark eyes. It was a *peri*, a fairy.

"Greetings," said the peri. "Follow me, I have good news." Then she pulled on her coat of feathers and flew into the sky.

✛

The old man stood up. His back was stiff and he brushed the dust from his robe. Then he followed the bird into the forest. The trees closed over his head. It was green and cool.

They went deeper and deeper into the forest. The trees were so thick, it grew dark, and the old man strained to see the bird as she flitted from branch to branch.

Then, in the distance, he saw something glittering. In the heart of the forest was a sparkling fountain.

The bird fluttered to the ground and pulled off her feathers.

54

"Drink and enjoy!" she said.

The old man drank. The water tasted good, like milk, honey, champagne, like pure clear water.

As he drank, the old man's back straightened and his dusty robe turned to shining green silk, green as new spring.

"This is the Fountain of Life!" said the peri. "Many have tried to find this fountain and failed. Gilgamesh went to the Underworld but couldn't find it. Korkut's search did not lead him here. Even Alexander the Great did not succeed."

The man laughed.

"But I wasn't even looking for it!"

"What were you looking for?" asked the peri.

"Wisdom," replied the man.

"The Fountain of Life," whispered the peri. "Now you have drunk these waters, you will live for ever. You are the water. And you will be known as *Al Khadir* – 'the Green One'. Whatever you touch will become green."

The peri pulled on her feathers and flew away.

✦

Al Khadir stood up. He felt young, strong and full of life. He picked up an old dry stick, and it burst into white blossom.

Al Khadir pulled the green robe about him and set off on his endless journey, walking through stories, wandering through lives, moving through prayers. With each step, the earth became green. And as he walked, he whispered, "Eternal life *does* exist. You are the fountain of life."

Al Khadir is still alive, bringing hope, granting wishes and helping those in trouble. Did you see him passing through the pages of this book?

55

About the Stories

These stories grew out of travel, talk and sharing. Like any storyteller, I have made the stories my own, while trying to pass on the spirit of the tellers who came before me.
Thanks for hospitality, conversations and help along the way to: the British Council; the British Museum's Striking Tents Exhibition; the BBC World Service Central Asia section; Stephanie Bunn; Gulnara Kasmambetova and all her warm extended family in Kyrgyzstan and the UK; Rose Kudabaeva; Alma Kunanbaeva; the Kazakh Embassy; the Kyrgyz Embassy; the Ismali Institute; Roza Otubayeva; the School of Oriental and African Studies; Valentina Tourabekova.

A Whole Brain – Kazakhstan (*Kaz-ak-staan*)
Alma Kunanbaeva was a wonderful guide and friend on my first visit to Central Asia.
She told a version of this story during her first visit to the UK.

The Secret of Felt – Turkmenistan (*Turk-men-i-staan*)
There are several legends about how felt was first discovered. All the stories involve water and pressure from feet or hands. In one version King Solomon is a little boy, has a tantrum and jumps up and down on a pile of wool. His hot tears and angry feet turn the wool into felt!
For more about felt: *The Art of the Felt Maker*, M.E. Burkett (Abbot Hall Art Gallery, Kendal, 1979); *The Arts and Crafts of Turkestan*, Johannes Kalter (Thames and Hudson, 1984)

Blue Sky, White Wing – Central Asia
I was always on the look-out for tales of the old, pre-Islamic gods Tengri and Umai Ene. I collected fragments of tales in conversations with artisans who made things from felt. They knew the old stories because they had been kept alive through the patterns and designs they created. Even the shape and constuction of the yurt symbolises the magical tree at the centre of the world.
For more on pre-Islamic religions: *Animal and Shaman: ancient religions of Central Asia*, Julian Baldick (New York University Press, 2000)

The Girl Who Cried a Lake – Kyrgyzstan (*Kir-giz-staan*)
Valentina Tourabekova is a superb storyteller with an endless store of tales. She shared many Kyrgyz landscape legends as we travelled through the country. She told me at least four different tales about the origin of Lake Issyk-Kul.

The Carpet of Dreams – Afghanistan (*Af-gan-i-staan*)
Storytelling needs carpets. A carpet defines the storyteller's space, like a stage, and creates an inviting place for an audience to relax. Stories are like magic carpets – they can carry you to other worlds. Some of the most beautiful carpets come from Afghanistan, and the idea that you weave a mistake into your carpet is an old tradition.
For more Afghan tales: *Folktales from Asia*, (Asian Cultural Centre for UNESCO, 1976); *Folk tales of Central Asia*, Amina Shah (The Octagon Press, 1970)

Riddle Bazaar – Uzbekistan (*Oos-bek-i-staan*)
Answers to riddles: Silk, Pomegranate, Snow, Onions, Wind, Needle, Moon, Tree.
For more Uzbek rhymes and riddles: *The Bread in the Sky*, Alexander Naumov and Oleg Stieffelman (Tashkent,1991)

The Bag of Trickness – Kazakhstan
Tales of Aldar-Kose are still very much alive in Kazakhstan. Everyone knows his name, and most people know at least one story about his outrageous trickery.
More Aldar-Kose tales can be found in: *Tales from Tartary*, James Riordan (Kestrel Books, 1979); *The Fairytale Tree: Stories from All Over the World* (Paul Hamlyn, 1961)

Zarina's Orchard – Tadjikistan (*Tad-jeek-i-staan*)
Central Asian folklore is a treasure house of stories about bold and brave heroines who fight battles, overcome demons and save their people from disaster. These heroines are powerful role models for girls growing up all over the world.
For more Tadjik tales; *The Sandal-Wood Box: folktales from Tadzhikistan*, Katya Sheppard (transl.) (Richard Sadler, 1971)

The Heart of Your Friend – Kazakhstan
This is my free interpretation of a Kazakh folk song. While it was being sung, Alma Kunanbaeva whispered a translation into my ear.

Father of Stories, Horse of Songs – Central Asia
This is a section of a much longer epic. Epics are an important part of Central Asian storytelling traditions, where tellers combine poetry, prose, speech and song. Performances last for hours, and even then a teller will only have told a small section of a tale!
For more on Dede Korkut: *The Book of Dede Korkut*, G. Lewis (transl.), (Penguin Books, 1974); *Oral Epics of Central Asia*, Nora K. Chadwick and Victor Zhirmunsky (Cambridge University Press, 1969)

The Fountain of Life – Central Asia
Al Khadir appears in many stories throughout the Islamic world. Sometimes he is accompanied by Alexander the Great or Moses. The man with green skin is also part of the Celtic tradition, and like Al Khadir, he is the god of the forest bringing new life. Al Khadir's name has a variety of spellings. You can find more about him in: *The Encyclopaedia of Islam* (Brill, Leiden, 1960); *The Koran*, Sura XVIII 59–81 (Everyman's Library, 1992)

For more on Central Asia:
A Traveller's Companion to Central Asia, Kathleen Hopkirk (John Murray, 1993)
The Hundred Thousand Fools of God: musical travels in Central Asia,
Theodore Levin (Indiana University Press, 1996)

Central Asia

Black Sea

TURKEY

Mediterranean Sea

GEORGIA

ARMENIA

AZERBAIJAN

Caspian Sea

EGYPT

Red Sea

IRAQ

SAUDI ARABIA

RUSSIA

KAZAKHSTAN

Karakum Desert

TURKMENISTAN

UZBEKISTAN

Samarkand •

Lake Issyk-Kul

KYRGYZSTAN

TADJIKISTAN

CHINA

IRAN

• Herat

AFGHANISTAN

PAKISTAN

INDIA

Persian Gulf

Glossary

Al Khadir – Islamic saint who drank the water of life. In paintings,
he always wears green

Angel Gabriel – appears in Christian, Muslim and Jewish mythology

Bazaar – market-place

Caravanserai – inn for travellers

Dasturxan – tablecloth or hospitality

Dev – demon or ogre that can change its shape

Dombra – Two-stringed, plucked lute from Kazakhstan

Erte, erte, ertede (Kazakh) – long, long ago

Ilgeri, Ilgeri (Kyrgyz) – once upon a time

Jailoo – summer pastures on the mountain slopes where the sweetest
grass is found

Kamchy (Kyrgyz) – whip

Karakum – "Black Sands", desert in Turkmenistan

Karaqul – black sheep with fluffy coats, also known as Persian lambs,
famous for their fleece used to make Astrakhan coats and hats

Kesh-kumay (Kyrgyz) – "kiss-the-girl", game of kiss-chase played on horseback

Khan – head of the tribe

Kobiz – bowed horsehair fiddle

Kumys – drink made from mare's milk. It tastes a bit like sour yoghurt

Nomad, nomadic – tribes that wander from place to place on a seasonal route
following their herds or hunting

Peri – fairy girl with wings who can take the shape of a bird

Plov – rice cooked with nuts, vegetables and raisins

Samovar – urn for boiling water and making tea

Steppe – flat grassland or desert. Much of Central Asia is steppe

Tengri – ancient god representing Father Sky, endless blue heaven

Umai Ene – ancient goddess representing Mother Earth, half-bird, half-woman

Yurt – round, domed tent made from a collapsible wooden frame covered with felt

My tales I have told them
Your pocket shall hold them
If they are bitter or if they are sweet
Carry them away and bring them
back—along with a dish of
rice and raisins.